JUMPING THE BROOM

by Courtni C. Wright

illustrated by Gershom Griffith

Holiday House/New York

Text copyright © 1994 by Courtni C. Wright
Illustrations copyright © 1994 by Gershom Griffith
All rights reserved
Printed in the United States of America
First Edition

Library of Congress Cataloging-in-Publication Data
Wright, Courtni Crump.
Jumping the broom / by Courtni C. Wright ; illustrated by Gershom Griffith.
p. cm.
Summary: Eight-year-old Lettie describes the preparations for her
sister's wedding and the day itself, a day of celebration in the
slave quarters, where free time for fun is infrequent.
ISBN 0-8234-1042-0
[1. Weddings—Fiction. 2. Slavery—Fiction. 3. Afro-Americans
—Fiction.]
I. Griffith, Gershom, ill. II. Title.
PZ7.W9348Ju   1994   92-45575   CIP   AC
[E]—dc20

For Stephen, my husband,
Ashley, my son,
Sallie, my mother,
and Phyllis Sidorsky, my dear friend

C.C.W.

To Ma and Daddy

G.G.

It is November. The leaves have turned red, yellow, and orange, and we have finished the harvesting. Life in the slave quarters has quieted down. The hardest work of picking, sorting, and bailing the cotton is over for a while. We usually work from sunup to sundown everyday except Sunday. On that day, we catch up on our personal chores or celebrate a wedding or birth. This Sunday, we will celebrate a wedding.

Many of the men are making furniture for the cabins from logs and twigs. Others are catching fish that they will salt for the winter. The women are cooking, sewing, and cleaning for tomorrow's wedding celebration. We call it "jumping the broom."

My big sister Tillie is the one who is getting married. I am so excited, I can hardly sleep or eat or think of anything else. My brothers, Peter who is ten and Joseph who is twelve, think all this excitement over jumping the broom is silly. That's because they'd rather be fishing with Papa when he comes to visit from Master William's plantation. They laugh at me and shout, "Lettie is dreaming! Lettie is dreaming!" as I walk by. They'll change their tune when tomorrow comes, and they see the food spread out in front of them. My oldest brother Sam won't be there. Master sold him away last year.

Jumping the broom is not just a wedding. It's a special day in the slave quarters. It's a time when all of us get together as one big family. We laugh and sing a lot. We tell each other about things that happened since the last wedding, burial, or birth. We don't usually have much free time for fun with all the long hours and hard work. The last time we had a special celebration was during the spring when Ben and Mary's baby was born.

People around here have been talking about Tillie and Will's jumping the broom for weeks. We have picked the best crops from the small gardens in the slave quarters and have cooked them for the big meal after the wedding. Everything is being kept fresh in the creek out back. We made money from selling garden produce to the other plantations to buy two chickens and a small pig from Master to go with the rabbits, squirrels, and venison we hunted ourselves.

We'll cook the meat on spits turned by the youngest children. The last one to turn the spit gets the first crunchy slice of venison. I can almost smell the food cooking. It makes my mouth water just thinking about tomorrow.

I'm too old for turning the spit. That's not work for an eight-year-old girl. For the last month I've been sitting and working on a quilt with the women. Mama said it was time I learned to sew. After the women finished toiling in the field or in Master's cook-house, and I finished cleaning in the big house and tending to Master's two children, we washed off the field dirt and grime and ate a quick meal of greens and yams. Then we met in one cabin or another—wherever there was a warm fire burning and a place to sit—and we sewed.

Mistress gave us a few of her discarded dresses for Tillie's quilt. Some of them had barely been worn. It's hard to cut up a good dress for quilt pieces when our own dresses are so patched and threadbare. When one of the women likes a dress that we are planning to use for a quilt, we happily give it to her and cut up another one instead.

We tried to pick dress cloth with flowers and bright colors. I wanted Tillie to have the best quilt ever made, so I picked out material with good texture, too. The different textures made the quilt feel good. When we used wool fabric, the quilt piece was rough. When we used cotton, the piece was smooth. Since it will soon be winter and cold in Tillie's new cabin, I tried to use many pieces from an old navy blue wool dress given to us by Mistress. Tillie will need a very warm quilt when the wind begins to whistle through the cracks in the cabin walls.

Tillie said that she wanted a star quilt with eight points on each star. She helped us select the pieces of cloth. Since blue is her favorite color, there are three shades of blue in every star. There are also many reds, yellows, and greens.

We made each star by stitching together seventy-two small diamond pieces. Next, we connected the stars to white pieces to form large squares. Then we sewed all the squares together to make the top of the quilt. We used a plain sheet of cloth for the bottom and stitched it to the top on three sides. Tillie stuffed a thin layer of cotton inside the pocket for warmth and stitched up the last side. With tiny stitches, we sewed through the three layers to keep the cotton in place.

We also made pillows, sheets, and a sleeping pallet with new, clean straw for Tillie's new home. We couldn't use feathers since Master and his family use them for their bedding. Tillie's pallet smells really sweet even if it is only stuffed with straw.

Sometimes as we sewed we sang songs about freedom. You should hear the voices of the women rise to Heaven as they sing or hum songs like "Go Down, Moses" and "Swing Low, Sweet Chariot." One of the older women named Hattie had to stop sewing to wipe the tears from her eyes. The voices were so beautiful!

While the women sewed, some of the men with carpentry skills made things for the cabin. They made baskets for holding crops from the slave quarters' gardens. Later, the baskets will hold the new babies. The men also made wooden cooking spoons, tables, and three-legged stools.

Many times in the last few weeks I have gone to bed tired but as content as one of the barn cats sleeping in the sun. We have worked late into the night. This is such a joyful time in the quarters, I don't mind being tired. After all, we don't have a wedding every day.

Bright and early in the morning the rooster crows, waking me from a sound sleep. I open my eyes and remember that this is my sister's wedding day. After dressing quickly, I sit on a stool and watch Tillie get ready. Mama has sewn a pretty blue cotton dress with puffed sleeves for her. Mama is the best seamstress on the plantation and makes many of the gowns for Mistress. Her stitches are so tiny that you can hardly even see them. Mama says that if I keep working at my sewing, someday my stitches will look just like hers. When the time comes, I can teach my daughter how to make the same tiny stitches, and then she can teach her daughter.

I can hardly keep from bursting as I join the other slaves in the yard. We are waiting for Tillie in the clearing in front of the quarters. What a beautiful fall day! The birds are singing, and the sun is shining brightly. The air is crisp and filled with the smells of food cooking. Mama has placed wild flowers in the two big plaits that circle Tillie's head. She looks like an African princess wearing a crown.

With Mama on her left and Papa on her right and a big smile on her face, Tillie walks into the center of the clearing where her future husband, Will, waits nervously. He chews on his bottom lip and shifts his hobnail shoes in the dust. As soon as he sees Tillie, Will breaks into a big grin and reaches out his hand to take hers. The eldest and most respected slave says a few words of counsel to them. There is no minister in the quarters.

Finally, it's time for Tillie and Will to jump over a broom lying on the ground. Mama says that the broom is for sweeping away their past lives as they begin a new life together. Grandma Sadie says it sweeps away evil spirits, too.

Everyone cheers, laughs, and sings, except my brothers who giggle into their hands. Mama and Papa give them a look that stops the giggles right away. The little children scamper from one person to the next. They have stood quietly by their mamas for the broom jumping and can't keep still any longer. As soon as we finish hugging and kissing Tillie and Will, we sit down to enjoy the meal.

The roasted chickens, pig, squirrels, venison, and rabbits are done to a turn, and the juices from a chicken leg run down my chin as I hungrily bite into it. I look at my brother Peter, and I see butter from the yams and biscuits glistening on his chin, too. We point at each other and laugh, but we don't stop eating. The food tastes too good to stop for anything.

Tillie and Will sit a little apart from the rest of us on stools in a place of honor just for them. She barely touches her food and occasionally gives him a special smile. His big, strong hand carefully closes over hers. They look so happy.

Soon it's time for us children to entertain the older folks and the bride and groom. My brothers and I dance and sing along with the younger children. Matthew, the plantation musician, plays the fiddle. He's the best fiddler in the area. Master hires him out for the white folks' parties and weddings at other plantations. One of the older men pulls out his Jew's harp and plays along with the fiddle.

Everyone claps wildly as my brother Joseph does a split in the dusty center of the circle. Checking his pants to be sure that they didn't rip, he quickly stands up and takes a bow with one hand in front of him and the other behind his back. He looks very grown up and kind of funny at the same time.

In the afternoon sun the men and boys pitch horse shoes. The girls play with corn husk dolls, and the young children chase each other in a game of tag. Young mothers with new babies sit in a circle and talk about their children. Older women sit outside the circle and knit. Sometimes they offer words of advice on child rearing.

As the sun begins to set and the evening breezes begin to blow, we gather on the grass and talk. The young children, tired now, rest against their mamas. Someone begins to sing a song we all know. We all join in quietly. One of the elders leads us in "The Lord's Prayer."

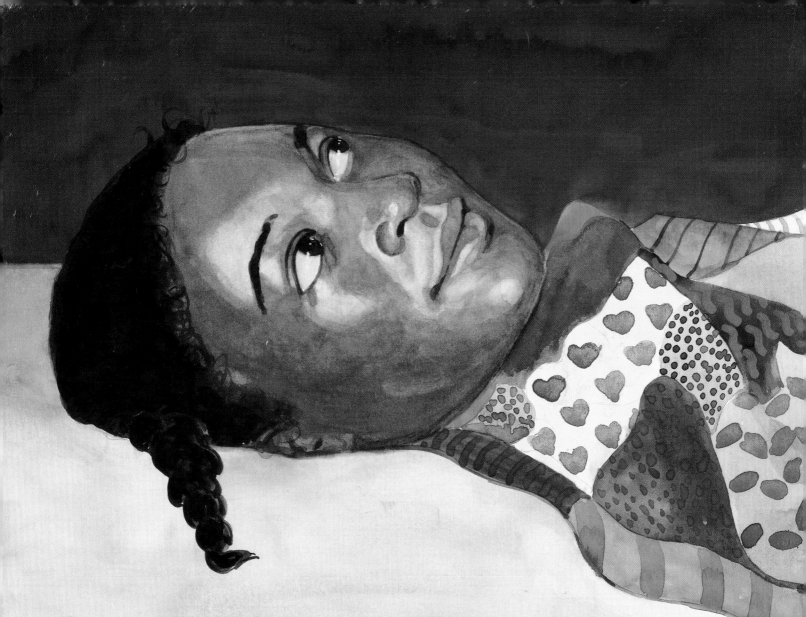

The day has gone by too quickly. Twilight comes and it is over. The first stars of the night twinkle in the sky. Work starts at dawn tomorrow morning. Slowly each cook fire is extinguished and every pot is washed. The last sleepy child is tucked in, and everyone says good night and goes to bed.

I lie on my pallet with my crazy quilt pulled up under my chin and look through a crack in the shutters at a little winking star. I feel lonely knowing that Tillie will never sleep next to me again. We have shared a pallet since I was born. At the same time, I'm glad because this was a special day for her and for Will and for all of us. I can hardly wait until the next jumping the broom!

E   Wright, Courtni
WRI   Crump.

             Jumping the broom.

$15.95

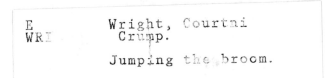

DATE			

BAKER & TAYLOR